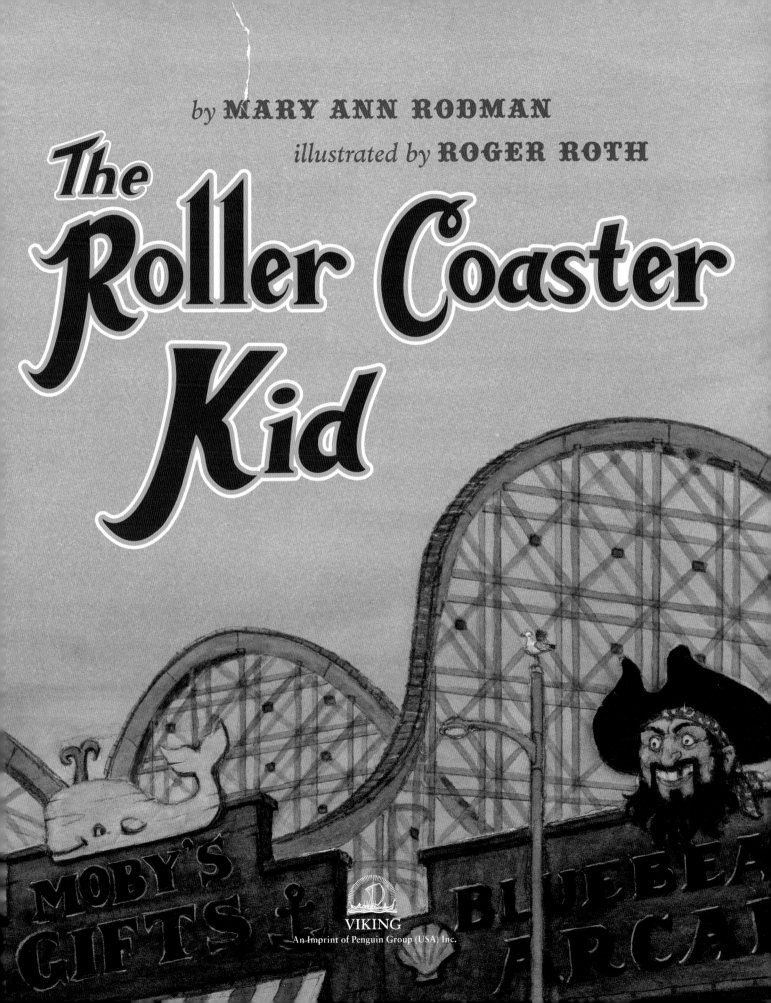

by **MARY ANN RODMAN**

illustrated by **ROGER ROTH**

The Roller Coaster Kid

MOBY'S GIFTS

BLUEBEA ARCA

VIKING
An Imprint of Penguin Group (USA) Inc.

J
PIC
ROD

**For Eloyd Baldwin and
West View Park (1906–1977)
—M. R.**

**For Harper and Astrid, with love
—R. R.**

VIKING
Published by Penguin Group
Penguin Young Readers Group, 345 Hudson Street, New York, New York 10014, U.S.A.
Penguin Group (Canada), 90 Eglinton Avenue East, Suite 700, Toronto, Ontario, Canada M4P 2Y3
(a division of Pearson Penguin Canada Inc.)
Penguin Books Ltd, 80 Strand, London WC2R 0RL, England
Penguin Ireland, 25 St Stephen's Green, Dublin 2, Ireland (a division of Penguin Books Ltd)
Penguin Group (Australia), 250 Camberwell Road, Camberwell, Victoria 3124, Australia
(a division of Pearson Australia Group Pty Ltd)
Penguin Books India Pvt Ltd, 11 Community Centre, Panchsheel Park, New Delhi – 110 017, India
Penguin Group (NZ), 67 Apollo Drive, Rosedale, Auckland 0632, New Zealand
(a division of Pearson New Zealand Ltd.)
Penguin Books (South Africa) (Pty) Ltd, 24 Sturdee Avenue, Rosebank, Johannesburg 2196, South Africa

Penguin Books Ltd, Registered Offices: 80 Strand, London WC2R 0RL, England

First published in 2012 by Viking, a division of Penguin Young Readers Group

10   9   8   7   6   5   4   3   2   1

Text copyright © Mary Ann Rodman, 2012
Illustrations copyright © Roger Roth, 2012
All rights reserved

LIBRARY OF CONGRESS CATALOGING-IN-PUBLICATION DATA
Rodman, Mary Ann.
The Roller Coaster Kid / by Mary Ann Rodman ; illustrated by Roger Roth.
p. cm.
ISBN 978-0-670-01150-6 (hardcover)
[1. Grandfathers—Fiction. 2. Fear—Fiction. 3. Death—Fiction. 4. Grief—Fiction. 5. Roller coasters—Fiction.]
I. Roth, Roger (Roger Almon), ill. II. Title.
PZ7.R6166Ro 2012
[E]—dc23
2011032976

Manufactured in China   Set in Minister   Book design by Jim Hoover

ALWAYS LEARNING   PEARSON

WHEN GRANDPA

was my age, he rode a roller coaster
one hundred times in a row.

DAILY RECOR

RID
100
ROW

A2

The Rollercoaster
KID

"My father's company picnic was at Oceanside Park," Grandpa tells me, as he shows me an old newspaper clipping. "All us kids got as many free tickets as we wanted, and I wanted a hundred!"

"The Rollercoaster Kid," says the newspaper headline over a picture of Grandpa, eight years old. He's standing in front of the big coaster, the Whipper. Except for his clothes, he looks just like me. We *are* just alike, except for one thing.

I don't like coasters. All that dipping and zipping and flipping makes me throw up.

Not Grandpa.

Every summer we visit Grandma and Grandpa in Oceanside.

We jump in the waves and find shells.

We feed the gulls and fly kites.

And we go to Oceanside Park.

Grandpa and I wait in line for the Whipper. This time I won't be afraid. This time I'll be the Roller Coaster Kid.

Then I change my mind.

"You don't know what you're missing, Zach," Grandpa says.

"Next time, Grandpa," I say.

But next time, it happens again.

"Never you mind," Grandma says. "Let's ride the Big Wheel."

Grandma and I like the same things. Seagulls and seashells and strawberry ice cream. But most of all, we love the Big Wheel. Easy and quiet, we sail up to the sky. Way up high, with gulls all around, I am not scared. I am braver than brave.

Down below, the Whipper looks as safe as a tiny toy train.

"Next time we come, I'll ride the Whipper," I say.

"When the time is right, you'll face your fear," Grandma says.

But that time never comes.

I'll never be the Roller Coaster Kid.

Next summer comes, but everything's different.

Grandma's gone. Forever.

We jump in the waves and gather shells. We fly kites and feed gulls, all our usual things. But without Grandma, it's just not the same.

Grandpa sits on the beach and feeds the gulls. He fixes our kite tails and carries the shell pails. But he's not like the old Grandpa, not at all.

He misses Grandma, and I miss her, too.

"We know," say my parents. "But don't say that to Grandpa. Talking about Grandma will just make him sadder."

"Let's go to the park," I say. "That'll cheer Grandpa up."

"No," say my parents. "He needs peace and quiet."

The Whipper, I think. That's what he needs.

Then one day, we're alone, Grandpa and I.

"Grandpa," I say. "Can we go to the park?"

He shakes his head no.

"We'll ride the Whipper," I say really fast. "This time I'll ride it. I really will."

Grandpa smiles. Not like he used to, but a smile all the same.

All the way to the park, my stomach hurts. I'm facing
my fear, but I sure don't feel brave.

There's a superlong line in front of the Whipper.

"Let's come back later," I say. Like never, I think.

"Nonsense," says Grandpa. "We'll wait."

We stand and wait for our turn. Before I know it,
we're getting on!

"Hop in," says Grandpa. *Clank!* The seat bar slams down. Trapped on the Whipper and I can't escape.

I close my eyes, supertight.
Clickety tick clickety tick. The coaster climbs slowly,
so slowly.
Clickety clickety clickety. Higher and higher.

For half a second, we hang at the top, then . . .

Whoosh! My screams fly away and my stomach does, too.

Hey, this isn't so awful. It's almost . . . fun?

But there's more.

Clickety tick clickety tick up the next
hill. *Clickety clickety clickety.* Then . . .

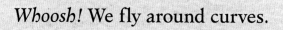

Whoosh! We fly around curves.

We fly upside down. Faster and faster. Down. Up.
Around. Over. *Clickety whoosh clickety whoosh.*
I keep my eyes shut.

Then it's over.

"Hey, Grandpa." I tug at his arm. "I rode the Whipper."

"Yes, Zach, you did," says Grandpa.

"So I'm the Roller Coaster Kid?" I wait for the big Grandpa smile.

"I guess," says Grandpa. He doesn't smile. "Let's go home."

My plan didn't work. I didn't help Grandpa at all.

We head for the exit. I walk slower and slower and get madder and madder. Didn't he know how scared I was? Why didn't he say "You were really brave, Zach"?

I miss Grandma.

Grandpa stops, and I know that I've said that out loud.

"What did you say, Zach?"

Oh no. I've made him feel worse.

I want to say "nothing," but that's not the truth.

"I miss Grandma," I say.

"So do I," he says.

"If Grandma were here, she would say I was brave," I tell him. "For riding the Whipper. For facing my fears."

"She would at that." Grandpa smiles his old smile.

He's not mad or sad, so I keep talking. "She'd say life's not so scary when you face your worst fear."

Grandpa looks at me for a minute, then says, "Your grandma was right. You are one brave boy, Zach."

We smile at each other. We're alike, Grandpa and I.

"How 'bout some strawberry ice cream?" asks Grandpa.
"OK," I say. "But let's ride the Whipper one more time."
And this time I keep my eyes open.